THE LITTLE TRAIN

by *Graham Greene*

Illustrated by Edward Ardizzone

The Bodley Head — London, Sydney, Toronto

All rights reserved   Text copyright © Graham Greene 1973   Illustrations copyright © Edward Ardizzone 1973   ISBN 0 370 02020 0
Printed in Great Britain for The Bodley Head Ltd, 9 Bow Street, London WC2E 7AL, by William Clowes & Sons Ltd, Beccles
Colour separations by Colourcraftsmen Ltd, Chelmsford   *This edition first published 1973*

The little train had lived all his life at Little Snoreing. From the day he was born in the engine shed behind the house of Mr Joe Trolley, the porter, he had never travelled further than the sleepy old market town of Much Snoreing, where the great main line crossed the little branch line.

Up and down the branch line, day after day, went the little train, punctual to the minute. Everybody set their clocks by him.

When old Mrs Trolley, the porter's mother, saw the smoke beyond the bridge, she said, "It's four o'clock."

Visitors in the warm summer weather would often leave the great main line and ride down the branch line to Little Snoreing. How often the little train heard them say, "What beautiful peaceful country and what a lovely sleepy village."

But the little train was sometimes bored to tears.

"Sleepy," he thought. "How little they know. Little Snoreing is fast asleep." And he would stand puffing at a level crossing, lost in a daydream. "If only," he told himself, "I could see the world outside where the great expresses go." One morning he had got up very early while his driver was still fast asleep. Suddenly he thought to himself, "It's now or never. I've enough coal in my boiler to take me to the end of the world." He thought, "Adventure, that's what I was born for. I'm just as good as an express."

Then he thought of his little warm engine shed and his
driver who was a kind man called Poslethwaite. "Shall I?" he
puffed. "Shan't I? Shall I?"

The porter who had got up early too couldn't believe his own eyes.

The foal who had been up since daybreak in the meadow laughed over his shoulder. "Poor little train, he's as slow as a tortoise."

The hedgehog who had just got up himself said, "Good heavens, he's going as fast as a bird."

The tortoise was halfway through breakfast and had his mouth full.

But with every puff the little train cried, "Freedom, freedom, freedom."

Meanwhile the porter had told the ticket collector who had

told the driver who told the stationmaster who telegraphed and telephoned to Much Snoreing. "Stop the little train. He's running away."

Too late. The little train was free. "Goodbye branch line, I'm going where the great expresses are."

You can see by the map on the next two pages of this book the way the little train travelled. At this moment he is just passing the spot marked X. He only went at twenty-five miles an hour, which is very slow for a train, but by midday he thought he had travelled hundreds and hundreds of miles. He was quite lost and thought that he might come to the end of England and see the sea. He had travelled through plains and hills and valleys and marshes and hills again. He thought, "If only the folks at Little Snoreing could see me now."

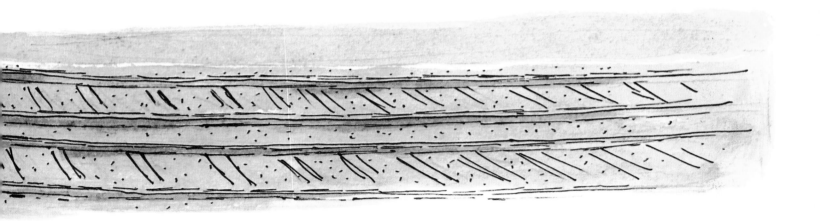

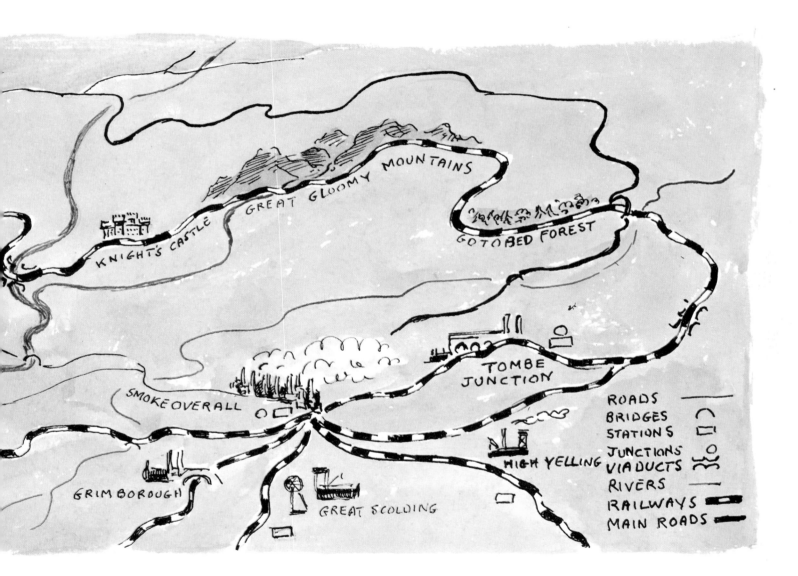

GREAT GLOOMY MOUNTAINS

KNIGHT'S CASTLE

GOTOBED FOREST

SMOKE OVERALL

TOMBE JUNCTION

GRIMBOROUGH

GREAT SCOWLING

HIGH YELLING

ROADS
BRIDGES
STATIONS
JUNCTIONS
VIADUCTS
RIVERS
RAILWAYS
MAIN ROADS

Once he saw an express rushing past on the down line and called out to him, "How are you, big fella?" but the express was going much too fast even to see the little train.

The little train passed over a big bridge and saw far below the steamboats going down towards the sea.

He passed a castle
where hundreds of
years ago a King was

put to death but the little train had never learned any history, he thought it was a new kind of signal box and hurried on in case they tried to stop him.

"Miles and miles and miles," thought the little train. He was beginning to feel very thirsty and sometimes he couldn't help longing for his nice water tank and thinking of explorers who had died of thirst in the desert.

As the sun began to go down the little train found himself climbing and climbing into the dark, gloomy mountains. There was no one there to watch him except the eagle soaring among the peaks.

In that desolation the little train began to long for the

friendly whistle of the guard, the tapping of the platelayers, the hooting of the little fog horn.

Here the only whistles were those of the big hunting birds, the only hootings . . . . . .

..... what was it that made that wild noise just behind his funnel?

Oh, how glad he was when the railway track tilted downhill and once again he could see the long, level plain. But little did he know what perils were yet in store. He had heard his driver

sometimes talk of junctions, but the only junction he and
Mr Poslethwaite knew was the junction of Much Snoreing.

Happy at having left the grim, dark mountains behind he

puffed through the darkening evening to the great city of Smokeoverall.

At first it was just a smell on the evening breeze, the smell of soot and oil and glue. Then it was a din of hammers and grinding brakes and shouting. Last of all it was a sight of blinding lights, huge black metal shapes, and more people than the

little train had ever seen in his life before, pushing, yelling. . . .
The little train in deadly fear shut his eyes.

Stop-Boomp-Woosh Mind your backs-OH- -BUMP-CLANG- -WHEE-BANG Grrr----

He opened his eyes.

Nobody had ever told the little train that the world could be like this. He thought that he had found his way to a terrible cave of demons. A huge voice that seemed to come out of the very air kept on repeating the mysterious words, "The train on number 3 platform is the midnight to Grimborough, High Yelling and Tombe Junction."

At Little Snoreing there had never been more than one platform, and in the maze of rails and platforms and cruel, shouting men the little train quite lost his head.

With a high squeal of fear from his funnel the little train bolted backwards. (Being on rails you see he couldn't turn round.)

The signals were all at stop, but the little train didn't even see them. The points switched him wildly from one set of rails to another, until he was reeling and dizzy. "Oh," the little train thought, "why did I ever leave Little Snoreing, kind Mr Poslethwaite and nice Joe Trolley. If only I could see them again, but I'm hundreds of miles away, I'm quite lost, I'll never see Little Snoreing again."

The stars which came out one by one winked at the little train like guards' lanterns, then one by one went out. The little train was quite exhausted. He had only a very little coal left in his boiler. When that was gone he would not be able to travel any further.

He would just come to a stop, until someone came and pushed him into a siding, where he would get older and older and rustier and rustier and nobody would remember him.

"Oh, I wonder," the little train thought sadly, "what new little train they will have on the Little Snoreing line. I wish I could warn him never to run away like I have done." And the little train's steam condensed into tears on his windscreen.

Rattle, rattle, rattle, that was the little train's couplings wanly creaking.

Puff, puff, puff, that was his little heart beating more and more faintly. There was only a shovelful of coal left in his boiler.

Woosh, woosh, woosh. What was that roar and rush bearing down on the little train?

It was the great Jock of Edinburgh, the famous Scottish express.

He drew up just in time, or else you would have heard no

more of the little train.

"Hoots wee mon," he said crossly because he was in a great
hurry. "What are you doing on my line?" The little train wept

and wept and told his whole story.

"Why ye poor wee train," said the great Jock of Edinburgh, "dinna fash ye'sel," (which is Scottish for don't worry).

"But I'm lost and I'll never see Little Snoreing again."

"Dinna talk rubbish," said Jock, "ye are only ten miles awa' fra Little Snoreing." (You can see by the map that he was right.)

"But I haven't any coal left."

"I'll push you hame ma'sel," said Jock. "We'll arrive there before breakfast time."

And sure enough before the clocks had time to strike seven there was the bridge outside Little Snoreing.

The little train's back

The little train looking behind him could hardly believe his eyes. Two tiny black figures shouted and waved their hands, they were Mr Poslethwaite and Joe Trolley.

The little train's come back!

"Goodbye, ma brave wee mon," said the great Jock of Edinburgh.

"Oh, I feel so ashamed," said the little train.

"Dinna fear," said Jock. "You're the bravest little train

they've ever had in Little Snoreing, and they'll be proud of you."

They were. The Mayor gave a reception and the little train was asked to make a speech. But his heart was too full of joy for words and all he could say was

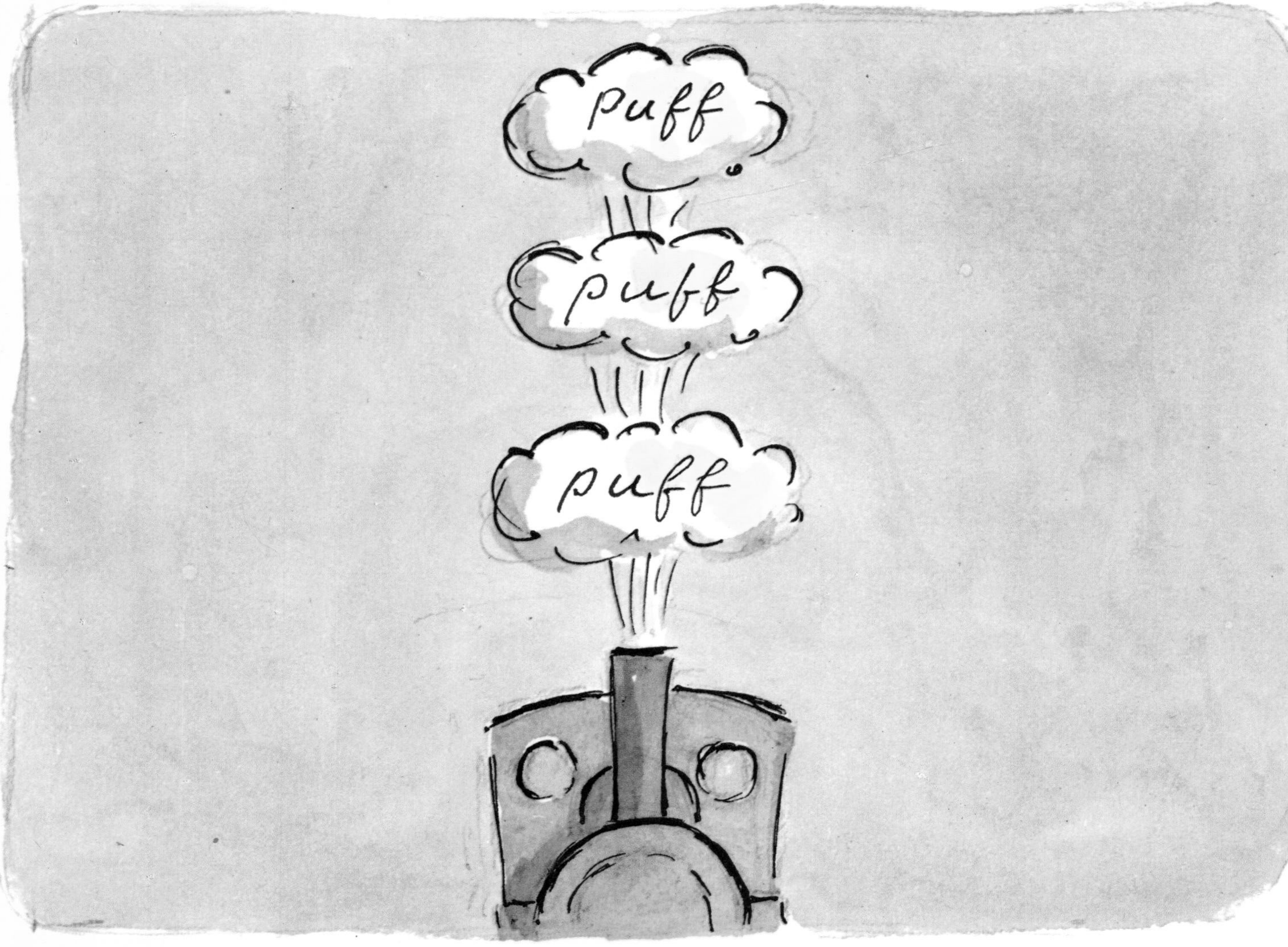
puff
puff
puff